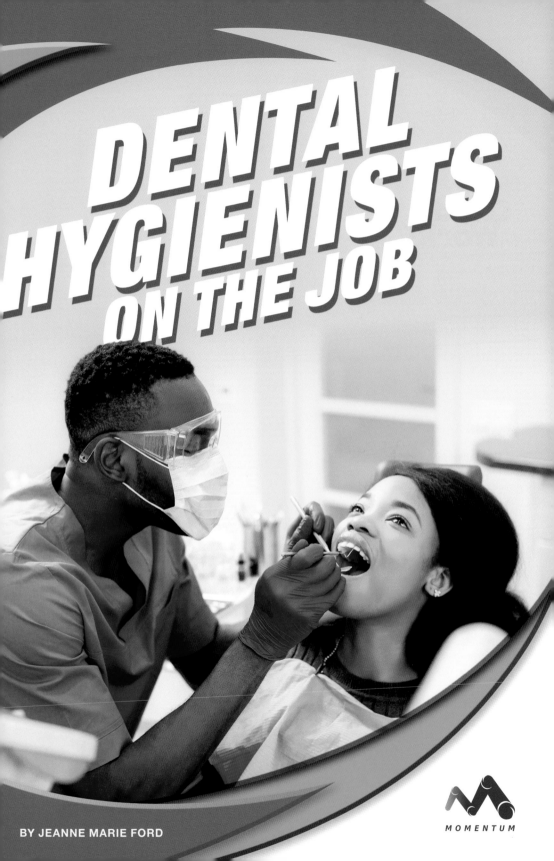

DENTAL HYGIENISTS
ON THE JOB

BY JEANNE MARIE FORD

MOMENTUM

Published by The Child's World®
1980 Lookout Drive • Mankato, MN 56003-1705
800-599-READ • www.childsworld.com

Content Consultant: Rachel Kashani-Legler, RDH,
RF, MS, Instructor, Department of Dental Hygiene,
Normandale Community College

Photographs ©: Shutterstock Images, cover, 1,
10, 22; Anna Jurkovska/Shutterstock Images,
5, 12; Ocskay Mark/Shutterstock Images,
6; ESB Professional/Shutterstock Images,
8; Katarzyna Bialasiewicz/iStockphoto, 9;
Sergii Kuchugurnyi/Shutterstock Images, 14;
iStockphoto, 15, 19, 21, 26; Avid Creative/
iStockphoto, 16; Lucky Business/iStockphoto,
18; Dirk Saeger/Shutterstock Images, 24; Joseph
Sohm/Shutterstock Images, 25; David Orcea/
Shutterstock Images, 28

ISBN 9781503835528
LCCN 2019942969

Printed in the United States of America

CONTENTS

MOMENTUM

FAST FACTS

What's the Job?

▶ Dental hygienists need to have at least an associate's degree, which is a degree from a two-year college. Most programs require two to three years of study. Some dental hygienists go on to complete a bachelor's or master's degree.

▶ Dental hygienists clean patients' teeth to remove **tartar**, also known as calculus, and **plaque**. They put **sealants** and **fluoride** on people's teeth to prevent cavities.

▶ After a dental hygienist finishes cleaning a patient's teeth, a dentist comes in to check the person's teeth.

Important Stats

▶ In 2018, many dental hygienists were paid around $72,910 per year.

▶ More students apply to dental hygiene programs than are accepted. In most states, graduates must pass a series of tests to be **licensed**.

▶ From 2016 to 2026, job growth for dental hygienists is expected to be much faster than for many other careers.

Dental hygienists check patients' mouths for ▶ signs of disease. They also educate patients on how to take care of their teeth and gums.

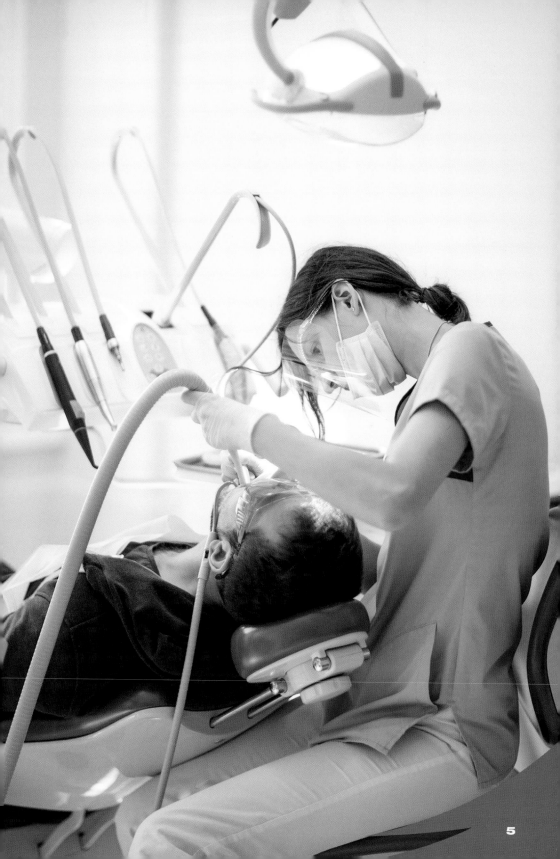

CHAPTER ONE

THE FIRST PATIENT

Maria hadn't felt this nervous in a long time. Today, she was going to see her first patient. Maria had studied for months to become a dental hygienist. She always wanted a job that helped people. Her favorite subject in school was science. She enjoyed her classes in chemistry and dental **anatomy**. She liked learning about how the health of a person's mouth could affect the whole body.

In school, Maria and her classmates practiced cleaning a mannequin's teeth. Maria paid careful attention to removing every bit of tartar from the mannequin's mouth. Tartar on an actual patient could cause tooth loss and damage to the jaw bone.

After a few months of working in the classroom, Maria was ready to practice on a real person at her school's dental clinic.

◄ **Tooth polishing can leave teeth feeling smooth and clean.**

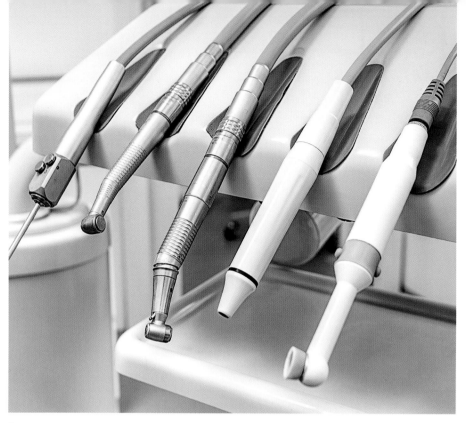

▲ **Hygienists use a variety of tools to clean people's teeth.**

The first patient she would see was another dental hygiene
student named Laura.

Maria washed her hands carefully. She made sure her work
area was clean. This was important to avoid spreading germs.
Maria put on her mask, gloves, and safety lenses.

As Laura settled into the chair, Maria put a paper bib
around Laura's neck to keep her clothes clean. She gave Laura
sunglasses to protect her eyes. She told a joke to make Laura feel
more comfortable. Laura relaxed, and so did Maria.

**Practicing on mannequins gives dental hygiene students ▶
good experience before working with patients.**

Maria used an ultrasonic **scaler** to clean Laura's teeth. The tip of the instrument vibrated quickly. The vibration helped break up the tartar. She pushed the scaler back and forth on Laura's teeth. The professor looked over Maria's shoulder and pointed out areas that needed more cleaning. Maria continued carefully. When she finished, it was time to polish Laura's teeth. Laura chose bubblegum-flavored paste.

Maria enjoyed making Laura's teeth clean and healthy. She aimed a jet of water into Laura's mouth to rinse off the paste. Then, she **suctioned** out the liquid. It made a loud swishing sound.

When she was finished, Maria removed Laura's sunglasses and bib. Laura ran her tongue over her teeth. She told Maria she did a great job. Their professor agreed. Maria sighed with relief. Tomorrow, Maria would take her turn as Laura's patient. She couldn't wait for her teeth to be smooth, clean, and white, too.

◄ **Scalers are tools used to remove plaque, tartar, and stains from teeth.**

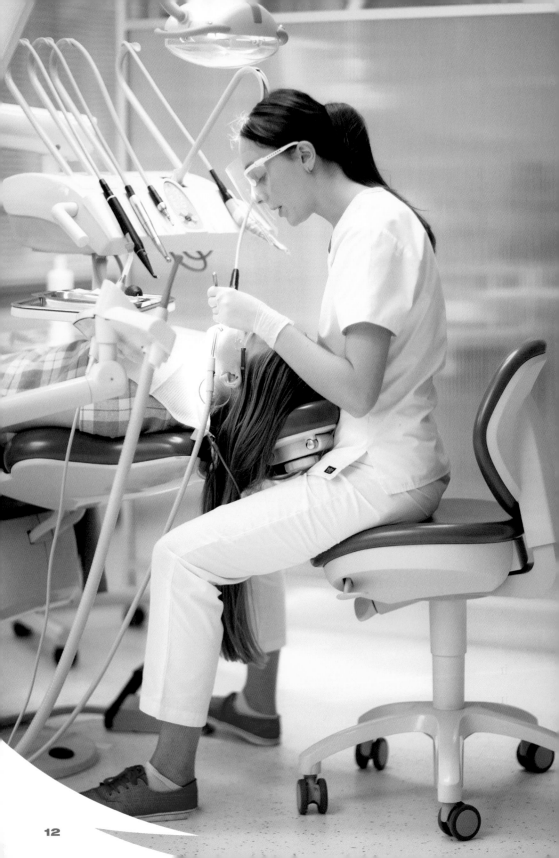

CHAPTER TWO

BECOMING A DENTAL HYGIENIST

Test questions flashed on the computer screen. Which nerves supply the muscles of the tongue? How does fluoride work to protect the teeth? John sighed with relief when he completed all 350 questions. He had been well prepared by his dental hygiene professors for this licensing exam. He had studied hard.

While John waited for the results, he attended the last weeks of his spring classes. He also prepared for one more licensing test. It was called the clinical exam. He would have to clean part of a patient's mouth at an exam site. John had cleaned many patients' teeth during dental hygiene school.

During the clinical exam, John's patient volunteer squirmed in the dental chair. Her jaw was tense. It was hard to move the instruments in her mouth. When John was finished, an examiner checked his work. John hoped he had done well.

◀ **Working with real people helps dental hygiene students feel prepared for their career.**

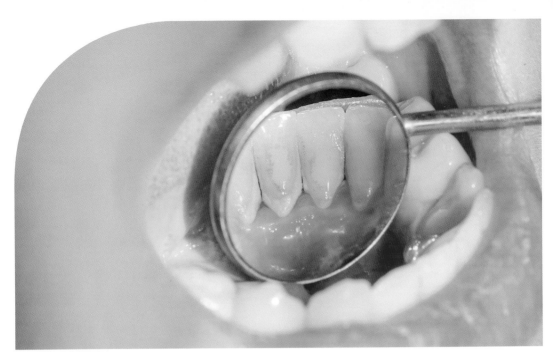

▲ **Tools help dental hygienists see the condition of patients' teeth.**

Several weeks later, John proudly marched across the stage with his classmates at his graduation. He had reached his goal of graduating from dental hygiene school. Now, he had to wait for the results of his licensing tests. He couldn't work as a dental hygienist until he had passed them.

Weeks later, John's phone buzzed with dozens of texts from his classmates. The test results had been posted. John logged on to the website to get his results. His heart sank when he saw the results on his computer screen. He had passed the written test, but he had failed the clinical one by two points. His examiner said he hadn't removed all of the tartar from the patient's mouth.

▲ **Dental professionals show patients how to brush their teeth properly.**

One of John's professors called him when she saw his results. She encouraged him not to give up. She helped him make plans to take the test again. He had to wait a month and travel to a different city to take the test. He also had to find another patient volunteer. John used the time to prepare. He was determined to pass next time.

A few weeks after the second clinical test, John learned that he passed with a nearly perfect score. He grinned and cheered with excitement. Now, he could finally work as a dental hygienist.

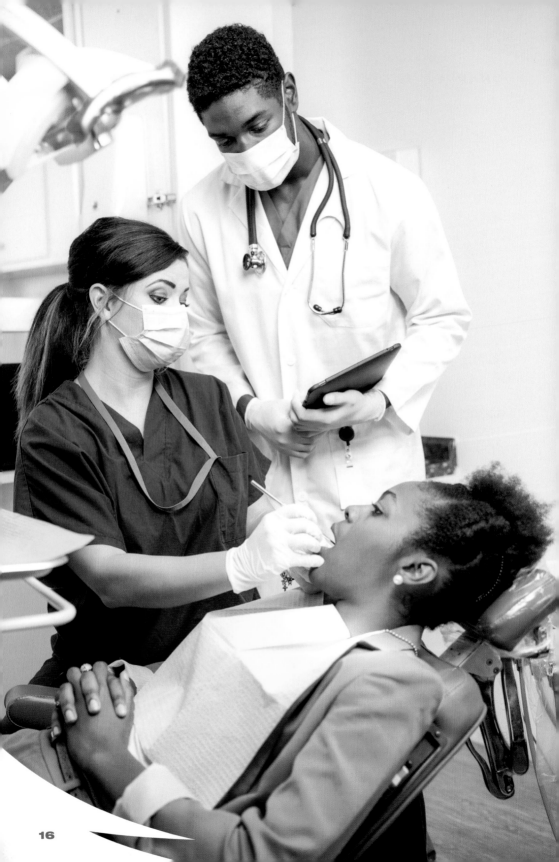

CHAPTER THREE

GETTING THE JOB

Grace's alarm clock rang at 4:00 a.m. She rolled over in bed and turned it off. Then, she rubbed her eyes and thought about the long workday ahead of her. Grace's first patient was scheduled at 7:00 a.m. Grace needed time to drive to the office, meet with her new coworkers, and prepare for the day.

After graduating from dental hygiene school, Grace took temporary jobs with different dental offices. One had eight dentists, and another had just two. One treated only children. One was a free clinic that helped people who couldn't afford dental visits. One treated military veterans. These jobs helped Grace figure out the kind of dental office in which she wanted to work.

Some of Grace's friends liked the flexibility of working in different offices. Grace knew she would prefer to work in the same office every day. She liked to have a predictable schedule.

◄ **Hygienists work with dentists to give patients the best care.**

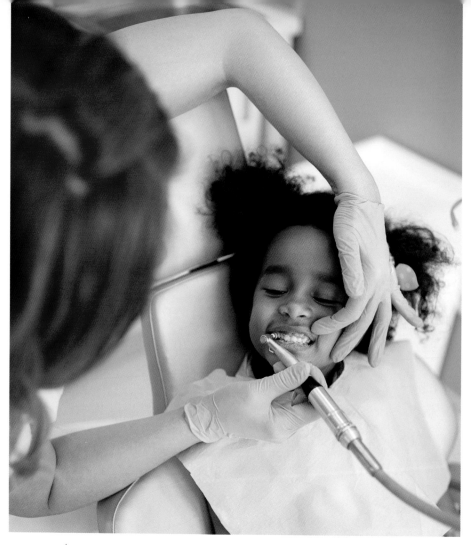

▲ **Dental professionals hope young children form good teeth-cleaning habits early.**

Grace also liked the idea of getting to know the same patients over many years. Today, she had a working interview at the dental office she went to as a child. It would be like an audition for a permanent job there.

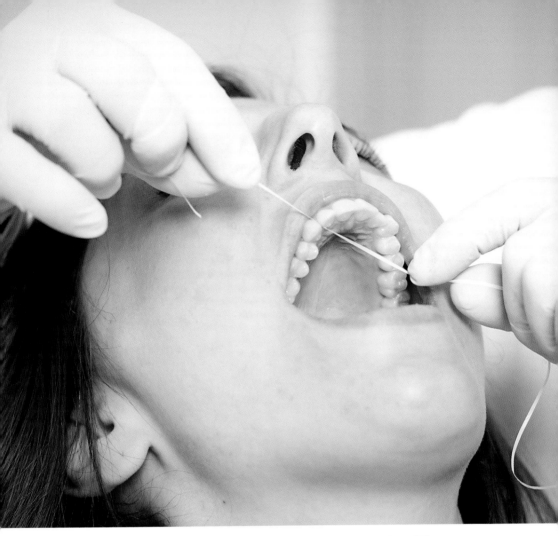

▲ Flossing helps keep gums and teeth healthy.

At the office, another hygienist named Whitney gave Grace a tour. She showed Grace the room where she would be working. She talked about how the office **sterilized** instruments. Every office had its own way of doing things.

Grace's first patient was a nine-year-old boy named Jackson. He had a bad toothache. It had kept him awake the night before.

He said he had trouble concentrating in school because of the pain.

After carefully looking at Jackson's teeth, Grace found what looked like a large cavity in the tooth that was hurting him. She told him that the dentist would most likely need to give him a filling. Grace explained that the dentist would give him medicine to make the area numb so he would be comfortable. Then, the dentist would use instruments to remove the **decayed** area of the tooth. Finally, the dentist would use a hard material to fill the hole and get rid of Jackson's toothache.

Grace found what looked like another tiny cavity that was just forming in one of Jackson's molars. Molars are teeth in the back of the mouth. Grace showed him how to brush that tooth with extra care. She explained that she would brush on fluoride and a sticky sealant to help prevent more cavities.

Grace talked to Jackson about how tooth and gum health could affect his heart, mind, and whole body. She and Jackson traded jokes as they waited for the dentist to come and look at Jackson's teeth. At the end of his appointment, Grace let Jackson pick out a green toothbrush and a light-up yo-yo. His mom made an appointment for him to come back to get his larger cavity filled. Jackson promised to take better care of his teeth so he wouldn't get another toothache.

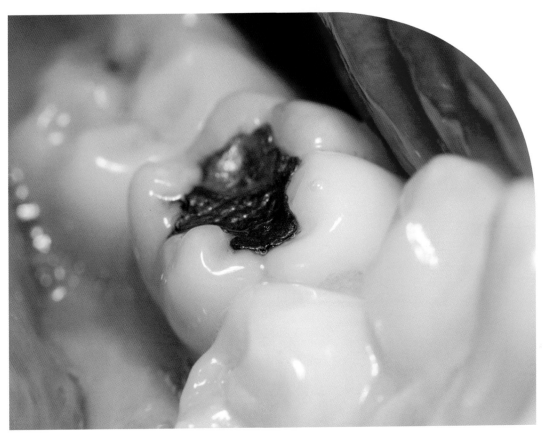

▲ There are different kinds of materials used for filling teeth. Fillings can be silver, gold, or white colored.

Grace was scheduled to work with eight patients that day. She had to work faster than she did in her college dental clinic. She also had much more independence because she didn't have a professor checking over her work. The day flew by. Grace worked for ten hours. Her shoulders ached and her whole body was tired. But it had been a great day. Before she left, she was thrilled when the dentist asked her to come back tomorrow to begin her new permanent job.

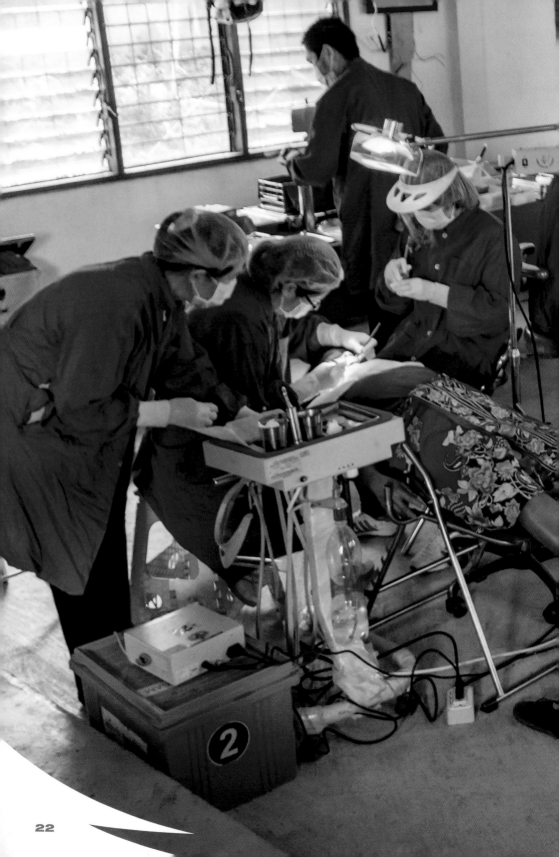

CHAPTER FOUR

HELPING PEOPLE IN NEED

Simone carried a heavy bucket of well water down a dirt road toward the dental clinic. The clinic where she and her American friends were volunteering was in a small Mexican village. It had no plumbing or electricity. Simone thought about the dozens of patients at the clinic. Most had never seen a dentist.

The hot sun beat down on the men, women, and children as they waited in line. Simone smiled at her first patient. The man looked down at the ground. At home, Simone always talked to her patients to try to make them feel more comfortable. But she spoke very little Spanish. The man spoke no English. Also, Simone didn't have many of the tools she used at home. She hoped she would be able to help him.

◀ Not everyone has access to dental services, so dental professionals volunteer to help people in different areas of the world.

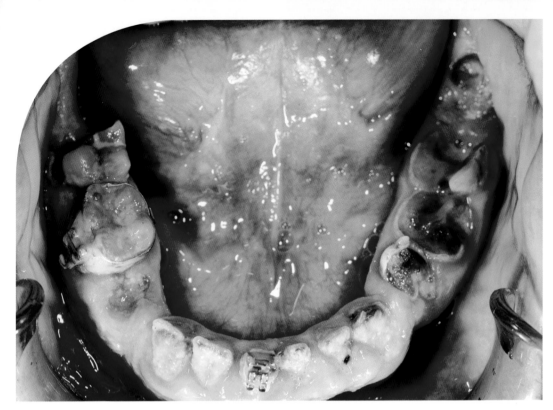

▲ **The bacteria in plaque can destroy teeth.**

A girl named Rosa asked the patient to sit on the ground. She told him to open his mouth. Rosa held the flashlight while Simone peered into the man's mouth. Several of his teeth were missing. The ones that remained were nearly black from the rusty well water he had to drink.

Simone removed the heavy plaque that covered the patient's teeth. She polished away the stains until his teeth were lighter. She flossed his teeth and his gums started to bleed. He rinsed his mouth with a cup of water. Rosa held a plastic cup in front of his mouth and told him to spit.

▲ **Free dental clinics help people in need.**

Simone gave the man a toothbrush and toothpaste. Rosa translated as Simone talked to him about how to take care of his teeth at home so that he would not lose any more teeth. He looked up at Simone and gave her a beautiful smile.

CHAPTER FIVE

MOBILE DENTISTRY

Shannon steered her mobile dental van into a nursing home parking lot. Many residents there were too frail or sick to visit a dentist's office. They would not receive dental care if she didn't come to them. Shannon grabbed her box of dental instruments and headed inside. Her first patient was a tall, thin man named Bill. He had trouble with his memory, and he rarely spoke. Lately, he had lost a lot of weight. His wife was worried because Bill didn't seem interested in eating. She wondered whether his mouth might hurt.

Bill did not want to get off the sofa. Shannon told him he didn't have to move. She looked inside his mouth and found the problem right away. A part of Bill's **dentures** had broken off. It was stuck in the roof of his mouth. Shannon helped his wife make an appointment with a mobile dentist to remove it.

◀ **It's important that people of all ages receive dental care.**

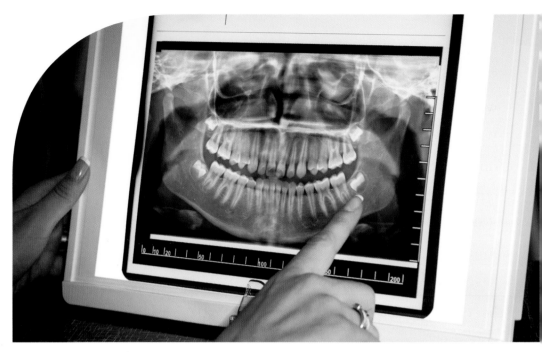

▲ **Dental X-rays can help dentists find cavities or decaying teeth.**

His wife was grateful. Once his mouth stopped hurting, Bill would be able to start eating again and grow stronger.

Shannon packed up her equipment and walked down the hall to see a white-haired woman named Ann. Two years earlier, Ann suffered from a stroke. Now, she used a wheelchair. Ann could no longer drive, and she had trouble holding a toothbrush. Ann spoke about her granddaughter's upcoming wedding. She wanted to feel her best at the wedding.

Shannon draped a lead apron over Ann's chest. She aimed an X-ray machine at Ann's mouth. Then, Shannon electronically sent the X-ray images to a dentist who was at a different location.

The dentist looked at the images and let Shannon know that there were no cavities. But Shannon saw that Ann's gums were swollen. Without regular cleaning, her teeth would start to become loose and might fall out. In addition to teeth problems, gum disease can lead to an increased risk of strokes, heart attacks, and other diseases. Shannon made sure a nursing home worker would help Ann brush and floss her teeth every day.

Ann was happy to have minty breath after Shannon finished her dental cleaning. For the first time in months, Ann put on lipstick. She had been embarrassed by her yellow teeth and bad breath. Now, she felt beautiful. She thanked Shannon for helping her, and she decided that she would smile in every picture at her granddaughter's wedding.

THINK ABOUT IT

▶ How can poor dental health affect a person's life?
▶ What qualities do you think a good dental hygienist should have?
▶ Do you think you would like to be a dental hygienist? Why or why not?

GLOSSARY

anatomy (uh-NAT-uh-mee): Anatomy is the science of the body's structure and how it works. Dental hygiene students must study anatomy.

decayed (di-KAYED): Decayed means to have been broken down. The patient's tooth had decayed without proper care.

dentures (DEN-churz): Dentures are fake teeth. Some elderly people wear dentures.

fluoride (FLOR-ide): Fluoride is a chemical that can help prevent teeth from decaying. Many patients receive fluoride treatments at their dental visits.

licensed (LY-sunsd): A person who is licensed has demonstrated the ability to perform a certain job. Dental hygienists must be licensed in order to work with patients.

plaque (PLAK): Plaque is a sticky substance that forms on teeth, contains bacteria, and can lead to cavities and gum disease. Dental hygienists use tools to remove plaque from teeth.

scaler (SKAY-lur): A dental scaler is a tool used to remove tartar and plaque from teeth. Dental hygienists are trained to use a scaler.

sealants (SEE-lunts): Dental sealants are thin, plastic coatings painted on teeth to help prevent cavities. Dental hygienists often apply sealants to patients' molars.

sterilized (STAYR-uh-lyzd): When something has been thoroughly cleaned to remove all germs, it has been sterilized. Dental instruments must be sterilized between each patient to prevent spreading disease.

suctioned (SUK-shuned): Suctioned means to remove liquid from a space by pulling it with the force of air. The dental hygienist suctioned the water from the patient's mouth.

tartar (TAHR-tur): Plaque that hardens on the teeth is called tartar. Tartar can cause teeth to look yellow and can lead to gum disease.

TO LEARN MORE

BOOKS

Hand, Carol. *Jump-Starting a Career in Dentistry.*
New York, NY: Rosen Young Adult, 2019.

Shaw, Jessica. *The Gross Science of Bad Breath and Cavities.* New York, NY: Rosen Central, 2019.

Wilcox, Christine. *Health Care Careers.*
San Diego, CA: ReferencePoint Press, 2019.

WEBSITES

Visit our website for links about dental hygiene: **childsworld.com/links**

Note to Parents, Teachers, and Librarians: We routinely verify our Web links to make sure they are safe and active sites. So encourage your readers to check them out!

SELECTED BIBLIOGRAPHY

"Dental Hygiene by the Numbers." *ADEA*, n.d., adea.org. Accessed 27 Feb. 2019.

"Dental Hygienists." *Bureau of Labor Statistics,* n.d., bls.gov. Accessed 27 Feb. 2019.

"Oral Health and Overall Health: Why a Healthy Mouth Is Good for Your Body." *Colgate Professional*, n.d., colgateprofessional.com. Accessed 27 Feb. 2019.

INDEX

ABOUT THE AUTHOR

Jeanne Marie Ford is an Emmy-winning TV scriptwriter who holds a master of fine arts degree in writing for children from Vermont College. She has written numerous children's books and articles. Ford also teaches college English. She lives in Maryland with her husband and two children.